Balamory

BBC

D0532724

The Sandcastle

RED FOX

"Oh, hi there. I know you, don't I? Did you know it's a play day in Balamory today?"

Miss Hoolie is in Pocket and Sweet's café. Suzie is bringing her a pot of tea.

"Good morning, Suzie. It's busy in here, isn't it? Look at Spencer's nephew, Calum. He's having fun painting!"

"Just like his uncle!" smiles Suzie.

"And here he is! Hello, Spencer," says Miss Hoolie. "What are you up to?"

"Hi, Miss Hoolie! I've come to take Calum and his pals to the beach. We're going to make a sandcastle!"

"So, where's your bucket and spade?" asks Miss Hoolie.

"Bucket and spade? Oh no! How could I leave my bucket and spade at home? I'll have to go back and get it. See you later, Miss Hoolie." Spencer dashes out.

"Bye, Spencer!" laughs Miss Hoolie. "Now which colour house is Spencer going to?"

That's right . . . The orange house!
  "Bucket and spade, bucket
and spade, where are you?"
  Spencer rummages inside
his junk trunk.
  "Aha! There you are!"

"Oh no! I mixed paint up in my sandcastle bucket and now the paint is all dried up and the spade is stuck to the bucket! Where *will* I find another bucket and spade?"

"I know!"

Pocket and Sweet's!

"Hi, guys! I need a spucket and bade – I mean bucket and spade! I need a bucket and spade!"

"Take it easy, Spencer," says Penny.

"Whatever's the matter?" asks Suzie.

"I promised to take Calum and his friends to the beach. We're going to build a sandcastle – but I don't have a bucket and spade!"

"Oh dear!" says Suzie. "Everyone wants to build sandcastles on this sunny day. I'm afraid I've just sold the last bucket and spade."

Spencer groans. "What *am* I going to do?"

"You could use a flowerpot?" suggests Suzie.

"Pity there's a hole in the bottom of a flowerpot?" Penny points out.

"Oh dear, so there is!" says Suzie. "And all the sand would fall through. That's no good."

"How about a dustbin?" Penny says.

"But it's so big!" exclaims Suzie. "Spencer doesn't want to build a sandcastle that big!"

"Oh, what am I going to do?" Spencer shakes his head. "Looks like I won't be building any sandcastles today after all."

"Wait, let's think," says Suzie. "Who might know how to make sandcastles without a bucket and spade?"

"Who is full of bright ideas?" adds Penny.

Archie is busy inventing a jam-spreading machine.
"Right, Nobby, let's try it one more time! Fire away!
YES! Perfect!"

"Hello, Spencer, fancy a jam sandwich?" asks Archie.

"No thanks, Archie, but I would like your help! How can I build a sandcastle without a bucket and spade?"

"Well, let's see . . . a yoghurt pot or jelly mould would make a good bucket, and for the spade . . . Ah yes! A plastic milk bottle."

Spencer is confused. "A plastic milk bottle?"

"Yes, look!" says Archie. "You just cut off part of the plastic milk bottle and use it as a sand shovel!"

"Amazing! Thanks, Archie! Now I have my bucket and spade, I can build my sandcastle!"

"Ah, but you also need flags, like the one on my tower!" says Archie.

"Where can I get flags from?" asks Spencer.

"You make them, of course! With coloured paper, drinking straws and glue!"

"Great idea, Archie! And I know just the guys who can make them . . ."

Calum and his pals get busy. They make lots and lots of flags.

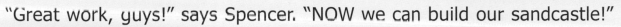

"Great work, guys!" says Spencer. "NOW we can build our sandcastle!"

Spencer, Calum and his pals make the biggest, most incredible sandcastle ever – thanks to Archie and his brilliant inventions!

What a busy day it's been!

Spencer promised to take Calum to the beach to build a sandcastle, but his bucket and spade was stuck together with old paint.

Penny and Suzie had sold the last bucket and spade, so Spencer went to see if Archie could help.

Archie found some yoghurt pots and jelly moulds to use as buckets, and he made a spade from a plastic milk bottle.

Then Calum and his pals made little flags from coloured paper and straws.

So, Spencer and Calum got to build a sandcastle after all, thanks to Archie's brilliant inventions.

And what a fantastic sandcastle! Don't the flags look great?

So, that was the story
in Balamory! Bye!

THE SANDCASTLE A RED FOX BOOK 0 09 947286 4
First published in Great Britain by Red Fox, an imprint of
Random House Children's Books by arrangement with the BBC
Red Fox edition published 2004
1 3 5 7 9 10 8 6 4 2

Text and illustrations © Red Fox 2004

B B C © BBC 1996

Balamory © BBC 2002